Dear President Obama

"Letters from Kogelo and Beyond"

By

Elizabeth Ochieng Onayemi

Mountain View Publishers

Kisumu, Kenya

This book was first published in 2015 by
Mountain View Publishers.

P. O. Box 2420, Kisumu, Kenya
ISBN 9966-7149-8-7

This book is dedicated to the memory of my dad
Prof. W. R Ochieng.

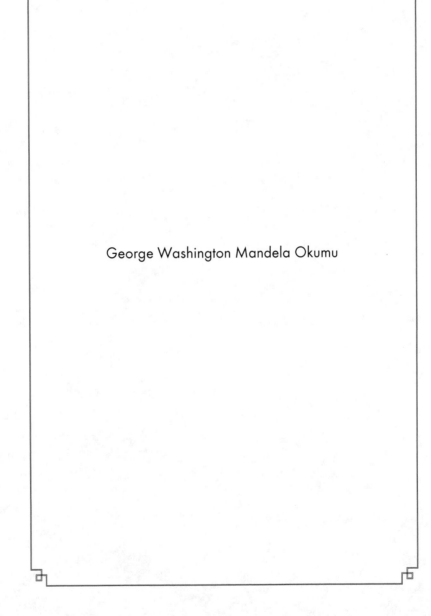

George Washington Mandela Okumu

Dear President Obama,

How are you doing? I hope you are fine. We are all okay here in Kogelo Village. As you know, this year the rains came, so the maize fields are doing very well. My friends and I are all looking forward to enjoying lots of roasted maize and boiled groundnuts during the harvesting season.

I'm sure you must be wondering who I am and why I'm writing to you. Let me start by introducing myself. My name is George Washington Okumu. My father gave me those names because he wants me to become a great president in the future.

Mr. President, I am twelve years old, and I'm a standard five student at Kogelo Primary School. I am a bit older than the other students in my class which is okay because I am a very short boy.

My mother always says it's important for people to introduce themselves properly, so I will tell you more about myself. As you know, all the residents of Kogelo are related to each other, so I am your relative. My great grandmother's sister was your grandfather's aunt's mother. Do you understand me? Luo relationships are very complicated.

Now I will tell you exactly where I live in the village of Kogelo although I know you've only been here a few times. Do you remember that old church with a rusty iron sheet roof? It's next to the maize mill opposite the primary school to the north of your grandmother's house.

To get to my house, once you get to the church with a rusty roof, take the narrow path that branches off the main road and walk towards the river. You can't miss that path because it's the only one, and it's right next to a huge mango tree. Walk along that path until you come to a house with a shiny iron roof, white walls and glass windows.

Your Excellency, my father is a teacher, and he built our house after saving money for many years. I hope you will visit us the next time you come to Kogelo. My mother only prepares delicious dishes when we have guests, so I hope you will come soon. I will understand if you can't come. My father says that you are a child of many worlds and belong to many people and many places. Not only Kogelo.

Now I want to share a secret with you. Please don't tell anyone about it. Remember what I said about becoming a president? Well, my dad wants me to become one, but I'd rather be a doctor. I think doctors are very important because they save lives.

When I was eight years old, I was so sick that I almost died. I had a terrible fever and a headache and kept vomiting. I sweated so much that my sheets were soaking wet. The village medicine man boiled some roots into a concoction for me to drink but it didn't help.

Finally, my dad rushed me to a hospital in Kisumu where a clever looking doctor in a white coat said that I had malaria and gave me some pills and an injection. I immediately felt much better, and a few days later I was back in class. It was on that day that I decided I wanted to become a doctor.

Mr. President, the day you became the president of the United States of America was the best day of my life. How we celebrated your victory in Kogelo village. I don't even remember what I ate, but I do remember that when I lay down to sleep that evening, my belly was so full it hurt, so did my feet from running around and dancing so hard.

I also remember that apart from dancing and feasting, we prayed that God would bless you and help you to make the USA, your country and the country of your mother, as proud of you as we are.

My mum always says that I talk too much and she's right. I haven't even explained why I'm writing to you. Anyway, here it is. I just wanted to wish you a successful second presidency. My dad says you're very busy. He also says that the world isn't too safe, and that part of your job is to work with others to bring peace to the world.

When I watched TV at our headmaster's house last Saturday, I realized that there are several wars being fought in different countries. Actually, even our own country Kenya is not as safe as it used to be and that's quite unfortunate.

Before I stop, I must say that I hope your country and other powerful ones will not forget poor countries such as ours because of your own problems. We need more roads, railways, schools and hospitals but have very little money.

Another problem is that almost half of the population of Kenya is jobless! My uncle is fourty and well educated, but he's never had a job. My mum says he's lazy, but I don't agree with her. I think the problem is that we don't know how to create jobs. Can you help us?

Mr. President, I know that I'm very lucky because my parents are teachers, and even though they are not rich, they take good care of me. Other children here aren't so lucky. They have no water, food or clothes, and some have no homes because their parents have died of Aids. Please remind the world to remember us, and urge our leaders to serve us honestly and diligently. Please reply my letter if you can.

God bless you and God bless America.

Yours Sincerely,

George Washington Okumu

Mama Magdalina Oyier

Sara's Grandson,

I greet you in the name of Jesus. I trust that you and your family are doing well. By God's grace, we are all fine here in Kogelo. After a long spell of dry weather, the rains finally came, so we are now busy working on our small farms. I am quite pleased with the outcome of my hard work because my vegetables are thriving. I've already made a few trips to the nearby market to sell cow peas and cabbages.

My grandson, I'm sure you don't remember me at all from your visit to Kogelo. I am one of your grandmother's best friends. We came to this village as young brides many years ago. We were beautiful girls then. Our eyes shone like hail stones in the dark, and our teeth were as white as maize. Our lovely dark faces were round, plump and as soft as cotton. Musicians constantly praised your grandmother. They called her jaber, Luo beauty. The two of us made a great team. Not only were we beautiful but we were also strong.

My son, in my youth my strength was celebrated all across Alego. I personally dug long stretches of land along the river. My gardens were famous for producing millet, beans, simsim, cow peas, sukuma wiki and sweet potatoes that were as large as a man's head. My kids never slept hungry nor did they walk around naked.

I sold my excess harvest and used that money to buy beautiful second hand clothes for my children all of whom attended the local school with your father Obama Senior and your uncles. All of them, except for my elder daughter Awiti who ran off to marry that wastrel Obongo. She should not blame me for the way her life turned out.

When I was recently informed that the residents of Kogelo were writing to you, I decided that I would not be left behind. I must admit that I am illiterate. I don't know how to write but I do know people who can. I said to myself, "Magdalina, the mother of engineers and big big important managers, your letter must be sent to America, to the White house."

I wondered who was going to write my letter for me, and then I remembered Siprosa. Siprosa my niece is a teacher at the local primary school and mother to George Washington Mandela a precocious but intelligent young boy known to us fondly as Awosi.

I quickly wrapped my shuka around my waist, tied my headscarf on my head, stepped into my rubber shoes, and hobbled off to Siprosa's house. When I got there, I learnt that she was away. She had gone to Siaya to visit her ailing mother at the district hospital. Fortunately, Awosi was home, so I told him what to write. I hope he has not changed the details of my letter. Children of these days!

Mr. President, I understand you will visit Kenya soon. I am writing to request you to bring messages of hope and encouragement to our people. We old people know a lot about the world but no one listens to us any longer. They've even stopped listening to radios. All they care about is television and the new thing they call the Internet. I've seen that Internet on my grandson's mobile phone. The one he uses to take pictures of me before running off to drink with his friends in Siaya.

My son, although no one listens to the old anymore, they listen to influential people like you so please teach and advise them. When we were young, when the British were here, things worked. Our country was organized. I used to travel by railway, all the way from Kisumu to Mombasa to sell dry tilapia. And then, I would purchase bundles of second hand clothes in Mombasa and transport them all the way to Kampala by train.

When the harvest was good, I packed bananas, vegetables, maize, smoked fish and ghee and sent them by train to my son Ogutu in Nairobi. Those things went by themselves. Without me. This cannot happen today. There are no passenger trains to Kisumu or Kampala. Is this development? There are no jobs for educated people. What is happening? When your dad came back to Kenya from America, he got a good job. Where have the jobs gone?

Everything we use is made in China. What's wrong with our hands that we can't make things? My grandson-in law from Japan could not open his factory in Nairobi because of government laws which an old woman like me cannot understand. Now, the Japanese has taken my granddaughter to Jinja to open his factory there. Wololo! If he had been allowed to open his factory here, he would have employed Jobita and all these idle boys in the village.

Sara's grandson, I will end my letter by wishing you well. We are proud of you. When your father returned to Kenya without you, we blamed him for throwing away our seed. Now we understand that it was part of God's plan. Because of you, the name of Kogelo is known throughout the world. Because of you, our young people now know that they too can make a difference.

My son, I told you that Mama Sarah and I used to be beauties. Now we are old women sitting in the shadows, but we remember the past with happiness. We pray that the future will be bright for our grandchildren and their children. When you come to Kenya, do remember to bring us old grannies some soap and sugar. That's what we tell all our children and grandchildren, and you are one of them.

Yours Sincerely,

Mama Magdalina Oyier

Kogelo Village

Oloo Mbuta Masembe

Dear Mr. President,

My father used to refer to your father as his brother, so you are my brother. Nyathiwa, we are proud of you here in Kogelo. When I heard of this communal letter to you, I decided to contribute. Unfortunately, I don't write well. I am a class four drop out and a failure to some people but not to all.

After dropping out of school, I herded goats for a while in Kogelo and then decided to look for life in Nairobi. My uncle who owns a bar in Kariobangi, offered me a job. I was sixteen years old then and thought that the opportunity to wash cars outside my uncle's bar was a godsend. In many ways, it was. The customers who were almost always tipsy, tipped me well. I used some of my earnings to buy flashy second hand clothes and shoes and sent the rest to my mother in Kogelo.

During my Kariobangi days, I didn't pay any rent since my uncle allowed me to sleep in the back room at his bar. I was never hungry since uncle also had a butchery adjacent to the bar, and the cooks gladly gave me leftover nyama choma and ugali. I became fat hence my nickname Mbuta. I was as fat as a big Nile perch. God bless uncle Otieno, Luo entrepreneur.

Cousin Obama, I am now a musician. I learnt how to sing by observing the Congolese live bands that performed at my uncle's bar. Although I was fat, I could dance very well. One Congolese band hired me, and the musicians taught me how to play the guitar and speak sketchy Lingala. That's how I left uncle's bar. He has never forgiven me. That's the problem with most people. When they help you, they expect you to serve them forever and they never let you forget.

Mr. President, I am now a resident performer at Club Limpopo in Kisumu. My band Orchestra Mbuta Stars performs a fusion of benga and traditional Luo ohangla. Our music mainly focuses on the theme of love in addition to which we praise beautiful well-endowed ladies. Sometimes, we sing songs in praise of hardworking Luo men and politicians. I don't consider myself to be tribalistic. As an entrepreneur in the music industry, I know that I must meet the needs of my fan base which happens to be predominantly Luo.

My band's music is all original with a few borrowed elements. However, this Friday, I will dedicate Onyi Papa Jey's song entitled "Obama" to you. Mr. President, this is a song about you, and you can listen to the original version on YouTube. Please remember to shake a leg as you listen to it in the White House. To anyone who doubts our ability to successfully perform Onyi Papa Jey's music, our response is, "yes we can!"

Best Wishes!

Oloo Mbuta Masembe

Brenda Emily Awino

Dear President Obama,

I hope this finds you well. My dad says I absolutely have to write this letter, and I must admit I think it's kind of cool. It's a great pleasure to write to you. My name is Brenda Emily Awino and I am part of your extended family. I don't live in Kogelo, and I don't visit that much although I know I really should.

My dad always says we should remember where we come from, and I do. It's actually his fault that I don't go to Kogelo that much. How is a fourteen year old school girl from England supposed to buy herself a plane ticket to Kenya and then find her way to a village in the middle of nowhere all by herself?

Now I know I've gotten you confused. My family is originally from Kogelo. When I was two years old, my parents came to England to enable my dad to pursue a PhD at Liverpool University. As he did his PhD, my mum studied nursing which is how we ended up living in England. My dad returned to teach Anthropology at Nairobi University, but my mum chose to work at a London hospital so as to give me and my siblings a better future.

My dad used to visit a lot. Unfortunately, my mum now claims that he's married another woman in Kenya and that his wife is doing all that she can to keep dad away from us. I don't know who to blame. Mum for insisting on living and working in London, or dad for insisting on teaching at Nairobi University and then getting lonely and marrying a second wife? Mum says he's absolutely never coming to our house in London again since she's not interested in getting Aids. I don't blame her, but I miss my dad and how we used to be a happy family.

I am currently in Kogelo attending my cousin's wedding. My aunt came to England and totally insisted that I accompany her back to Kenya to attend this function. The wedding will take place this Saturday, and I can hardly wait. All the bridesmaids are really fun, and we've had the greatest time ever. My grandmother Magdalina is really funny, and she's an amazing cook. My distant cousin George Washington is giving me Luo lessons, and I am already using some simple phrases to communicate with people. My siblings will be so jealous when I speak to mum in Dholuo in London. We are all so Cockney, you couldn't tell we had a drop of Luo blood.

Dear President, your presidency has been so amazing but also so confusing to us your clan. We are so proud of you and also so sensitive because your challenges are in many ways ours. My classmates in London always ask me about "Obamacare" even though they clearly don't understand what it's all about, and nor do I.

Kenya is still the same. I think some people secretly hoped it would change with you in the White House. I wonder how that was supposed to happen. Like I said it's confusing. I am totally confused because I'm not even sure if I'm Kenyan or British. I have a British passport. I still think of myself as Kenyan, but I love my new country. I don't think anyone like me could ever become a British Obama, and that makes me sad.

Mr. President, I will return to England soon after our cousin's wedding. I'm sure you don't know her. You would like her if you met her. She's a doctor. The first female doctor from Kogelo. Fancy that! She's really kind, smart and incredibly funny. She works at Siaya District Hospital, and has started this NGO called Siaya Girl Child Foundation whose aim is to provide scholarships to enable girls from poor families to go to university. I plan to do a gap year at this foundation after high school if my mum lets me.

I wish you a pleasant visit to Kenya later this year.

Your Cousin

Awino

John Kamau

Dear Mr. President,

I hope this finds you well. From my name, you can tell that I'm not from Kogelo, nor am I Luo. I work at the post office in Siaya. When I saw the envelope addressed to you, I could not resist opening it to slip in my very own message. I am a Kenyan citizen and I can relate to the people of Kogelo. I have lived in Luo land since I was a little boy and speak fluent Dholuo.

Prior to the fateful Kenyan elections in 2007, my parents were established charcoal dealers in the Nyalenda slums of Kisumu. I grew up playing football with barefooted Luo boys. We all wore ragged clothes and had permanent trails of mucus running down our noses simply because we couldn't be bothered to clean up. Our lunch consisted of dry omena fish and maize meal ugali. How I miss those days!

Heh! Mr. President, I want to narrate my post- election violence experience to you. The fateful elections happened when I was already working at the Siaya Post Office. When the media started featuring news of the escalating tribal clashes, I quickly boarded a matatu from Siaya to Kisumu. I knew that my old parents needed me because they lived in a slum surrounded by Luo people. Everyone in Nyalenda knew my dad Kamau. They all referred to him as Ja Kikuyu and sent their kids to Ja Kikuyu's to buy charcoal. As such, I sensed that he would become an instant target.

As the matatu sped towards Kisumu, I kept reciting Hail Mary's silently. My long forgotten Catholic faith was streaming back rapidly in my hour of need and great desperation. I kept my cap over my head to conceal my light skinned forehead because I did not want the other passengers to sense that they had a Jamua (foreigner) in their midst. The conversation all around me in the matatu was about violence, tribalism and retaliation. One scary looking character whose front teeth were missing kept emphasizing how he would personally skin alive any Jarabuon (potato guy) meaning Kikuyu he came across. Haiya!

Mr. President, the moment the matatu arrived at the Kisumu bus stop, I quickly jumped out and got onto a boda boda motorbike. I shouted quickly, "Nyalenda Buddies Bar." Without hesitating, the boda driver sped off in the general direction of Nyalenda. Tension and confusion were evident everywhere. We met crowds of individuals lagging heavy furniture and equipment looted from Indian stores downtown with policemen hard on their heels with tear gas.

The crowd kept hurling rocks at the policemen and lagging their looted booty. The boda cyclist artfully dodged the rioting looting crowd and kept riding in the direction of Nyalenda. I glimpsed smoke billowing out of what used to a major supermarket in the city center. As I stared backwards, a bullet came whistling through the air and narrowly missed my ear. Mwadhani!

At that point, the boda decided that he could go no further. He ordered me to get off the bike and zoomed away without even collecting his fare. Fortunately, I was now just a few minutes away from my parent's home. I maneuvered my way through the rioting crowds, and found my way to my parent's house. When I got there, I could not believe my eyes. The house was no more. It had been razed to the ground. The charcoal yard had likewise been levelled down, and all the sacks of charcoal had been looted. The only evidence that charcoal had ever been sold on that spot was the black charcoal dust that lay on the ground. Uwi!

Trying to control my tears, I crept into Mama Akeyo's house. She was my mother's best friend, and I knew she wouldn't betray me to the angry neighbors. Mama Akeyo jumped up and gave me a hug glancing furtively behind me and bolting her door shut. Whispering into my ear, she said, "don't worry about your parents. We bundled them out of here two days ago. They are hiding out in our village home in Nyakatch up in the hills. No one knows they are there. They will be safe."

I was so relieved to hear that. Tears of joy run down my cheeks. Mama Akeyo asked me to hide under her bed until later that evening when a mysterious boda cyclist came and whisked me to safety, up to the hills of Nyakatch where my parents had sought refuge.

A week later, we traveled to our rural homestead in Kiambu using backroads. On the way, we witnessed angry Kikuyus unleashing violence on Luos and Luhyias in Naivasha. We realized that Kenyans had gone crazy. We got to Kiambu safe but traumatized. We didn't like it one bit. We are Luos at heart. We'd lived in Luo land for too long and had forgotten how to be Kikuyus.

Mr. President, the dust has since settled. I returned to my job in Siaya. Dad and mum were too traumatized to return to Kisumu. Since they were used to living in a more tribally diverse community, they decided to settle in the Kawangware slums of Nairobi where they now live happily amongst Luos, Luhyias, Kikuyus and other Kenyan tribes.

I almost married a Luo Lady but she dumped me so I'm still looking. There's a nice looking Kisii hairdresser in the salon next door. I'm thinking of asking her out this coming Friday. Orchestra Mbuta Stars is coming to town. And yes, I enjoy ohangla music.

Yours Sincerely,

John Kamau

Reverend Owiti

Dear Brother Obama,

Praise the Lord! Praise the name of the living God. President, I know that you are a true believer, so I want to thank God for your leadership. God in his blessed and everlasting grace has placed you in your position of power and privilege. You are a living testimony to all those unbelievers and doubting Thomases who assumed that never would a black man live and reign in the White House. We thank God for you Brother Obama.

My name is Reverend Bob Owiti. I hail from the Kano plains of Western Kenya. I trained in Theology in Uganda and returned home to serve the Lord. I am now a reverend here in Nyangoma Sub Parish. I feel called to reveal the gospel to the people of Kogelo and surrounding villages. Heh! Evangelizing in rural Kenya is not an easy job. Some of our people here have impenetrable hearts of stone. Many are addicted to changaa and busaa. Others are involved in witchcraft and night running. My honorable brother, it's not easy.

Last week, I was caught up in a serious confrontation between a local leader and his two wives, each of whom was accusing the other of bringing Aids to the family. I am not one to point fingers, but I think these people should act responsibly. I plan to counsel them all accordingly. And to think that the man used to be a pastor at our church before marrying the second wife! It's hard but God will help us.

Before I stop, I want to request you to find a sponsor for our church. We have ambitious plans to build a huge cathedral in our sub parish. A towering church that will put others to shame. This cathedral will win hundreds of souls. I myself take ownership of this vision and trust that it will come to pass by God's grace.

Amen! Hallelujah!

Reverend Owiti

Mark Omondi

Dear Mr. President,

I am a class one student in Kogelo and here is my poem to you:

One, two, three, four, five

I like America

Six, seven, eight, nine, ten

I am from Africa

What do you want to be?

I want to be a president.

Which country will you rule?

Every country in the world.

Yours Sincerely,

Mark Omondi

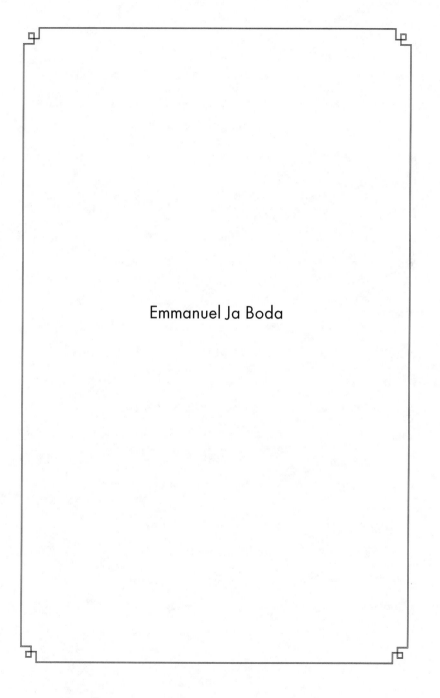

Emmanuel Ja Boda

Dear President Obama,

Yawa! I hope you are doing very well my brother. I am fine here at Nyangoma Market where I do my boda boda motorbike taxi business. They call me Emmanuel Ja Boda because I am a boda boda cyclist. I am your clan mate which means we're descended from the same family branch. We share a common great grandfather, and I ja boda am your very brother by blood. Our families cannot intermarry. It's strictly forbidden in our culture. Such a thing cannot happen because we are brothers and sisters. Same blood.

I came to find out about these letters that are being sent to you quite by accident. I was carrying that old madhe Magdalina on my boda from the market when she asked me to stop by Reverend Owiti's house. She did not want to get off the boda ,so she asked me to hoot loudly which I did. The Reverend came out and greeted her saying, "Yes madhe, praise God." The madhe said, "Amen pastor." The pastor said, "Eh, I have finished writing that letter to Obama and will deliver it to the teacher later today."

At that moment I started wondering what they were discussing, and which Obama the letter had been written to. The Obama in Kogelo, one of the ones abroad, or the president yawa? "Did you tell him about the church we want to build?" asked the madhe. "Yawa, how can I forget such an important message!" exclaimed the reverend.

At that point, the madhe was satisfied and she bid the reverend goodbye.

Later that day, I met George Washington standing under that mango tree that leads to his home. That boy and mangoes! No wonder he's so chubby. His stomach is full of mangoes. Despite being so young, Awosi knows everything that's worth knowing in our village. He's so clever. He'll be a professor one day. Anyway, I asked Awosi if he knew anything about the reverend writing a letter to one of the Obamas. That's when he told me that village members were writing to you.

Mr. President, I was so annoyed. "How can these people write so many letters to you and not include mine?" As I said before, we are descended from the same great grandfather. They are joking with me. I may be a boda cyclist but I'm very intelligent and independent. I don't ask anyone for anything. I feed myself and my children. My first born is in form one at Maranda Boys High School, and I paid all his school fees in cash. Let them not joke with me.

I told Awosi, "If you post those letters without including mine, you will see me!" The boy started trembling. I pointed at him and then sped off on my boda boda.

Anyway, Mr. President, I just want to welcome you to Kenya later this year. As you know, we are peace loving and God fearing people.

The request I have from the boda cyclists at Nyangoma Kogelo is that you ask our government to go easy on taxes. Eih! Petrol is very expensive now and the county government is collecting too much money from us here at the market. They must think we're just plucking money from trees.

Boda boda business is hard. Sometimes we carry old madhes and when they reach their destination they claim not to have money. Sometimes we carry thugs who steal all our money. Sometimes we carry girls who think they can flirt with us for free rides. And then people think we are a nuisance. I think we should all go on strike, and let them walk for those many kilometers they used to walk before boda bodas arrived on the scene.

My brother, we'll talk one day.

Peace and Prayer!

Emmanuel Ja Boda

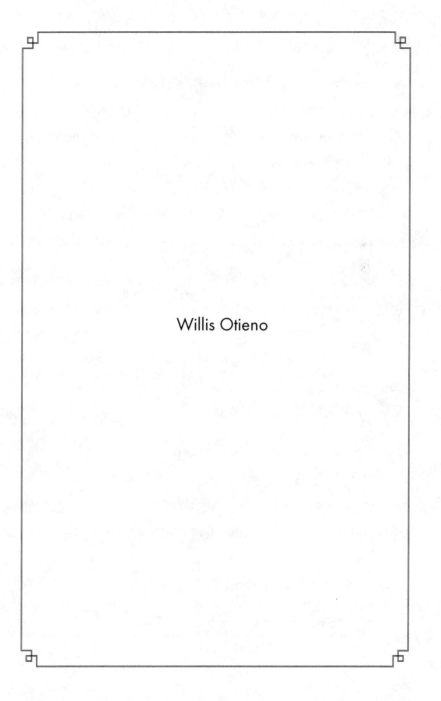

Willis Otieno

Dear President,

How are you? I hope you're fine. My name is Willis Otieno and I am one of the Baghdad Boys from Kondele in Kisumu. People refer to us as political thugs associated with the Luo political leadership, but those are false claims. We are modern day Luo warriors, and our fight is not one for political or tribal supremacy but rather a peaceful struggle for recognition, equality, and a right to the Kenyan political cake.

On ordinary days, we are a bunch of noisy but peaceful Kenyan citizens who work hard to earn a living touting, selling pirated DVDs, transporting Kenyans on boda bodas, washing cars, panel beating and generally doing a variety of jobs in the Kondele, Manyatta and Kibuye areas. But make no mistake, when someone steps on our political toes, all hell breaks loose.

Note that we are not trouble makers. When President Uhuru Kenyatta recently visited Kisumu, we welcomed him with open arms. The welcome we gave him was very different from that accorded to his father by our fathers and grandfathers, the now retired Baghdad Boys of the past. That is all in the past. We love Uhuru and we will work with him to develop Kenya.

President Obama, in addition to being a Baghdad Boy, I am one of your brethren from Kogelo through my mother's side of the family. My mother is from your very own village. My uncles gave me a piece of land to cultivate in Kogelo, and I make an annual pilgrimage to Kogelo from Kisumu to plant sweet potatoes, cassava, maize, beans and groundnuts on that land. Yes, Baghdad Boys can also farm. Like I said before, we are hardworking Kenyan citizens.

I recently came to Kogelo, my uncle's village, to oversee the weeding of my garden. During my stay in Kogelo, my cousins invited me to participate in the letter writing that was ongoing, so I decided to use this platform to positively represent the Baghdad Boys whose exploits have no doubt reached the White House.

Mr. President, I just want to reiterate that Baghdad Boys are hardworking peaceful modern day Luo tribal warriors. Other tribes have theirs. It's part of our cultural heritage as Africans. Unlike in the past where we Baghdad Boys used stones of varying sizes to battle out issues, we are now committed to using dialogue to verbally iron out national and regional issues. We urge warriors from other tribes to do the same.

People blame us for participating in the postelection tribal violence but who saw us? Your honor, Kenyans simply went mad during that time. Friends and neighbors turned against each other. The most dignified people behaved like animals. We warriors were taken aback. We also lost loved ones and belongings.

Our message to you and other global leaders is that Kenyans have put their violent past behind them. We are committed to creating and maintaining peace and unity in this beautiful land that God has given us. Luos are and always have been ready to collaborate with other Kenyan tribes.

God bless you and the work of your hands.

Your Cousin

Willis Otieno

Takahashi Hashimoto

Dear President Obama,

Mine is a very short letter written under extreme pressure from my grandmother- in -law Magadalina who I am currently visiting in Kogelo. My name is Takahashi Hashimoto, and I am a Japanese national now resident in East Africa. I came to Kenya to work for JICA (Japanese International Cooperation Agency) in the nineties. I am an agronomist by profession, and JICA brought me here to explore potential opportunities in agribusiness. During my stint with JICA in Nairobi, I met a lovely Luo lady named Nancy who happens to be from your clan. We fell in love, got married and now have three lovely kids.

Mr. President, I have since stopped working for JICA, and recently set up my own Sunflower Oil manufacturing plant in Jinja, Uganda. Why Jinja? Well, soon after marrying your cousin, and deciding to settle down in East Africa, I realized how unfriendly Kenyan laws were to male spouses of Kenyan females.

I had initially assumed that I could get a residency permit and permission to work or operate a business in Kenya by virtue of having married a Kenyan woman. That wasn't the case. The immigration authorities treated me like an unwanted and unfriendly alien, and stated categorically that I should take my wife away to Japan stating that in Kenya women don't marry men.

At that point, I decided that Uganda was a good option and indeed it has turned out to be. I was able to register my business here with minimal stress, and I'm now as happy as can be raking in increasingly handsome sums of money. I expect to break even next year after which the sky is the limit. Ugandan sunflower farmers are collaborating with me and oil production has shown a steady increase.

I am loving it in Uganda. If you ever visit Uganda, don't hesitate to visit my factory. We are pretty close to the source of the Nile in Jinja. We have a lovely house with a fantastic view of the Nile, and my wife and daughters would be delighted to host you and your beautiful family.

Dear president, I still dream of opening a small factory in Kenya in addition to which I look forward to the day when foreign male spouses of Kenyan women will be recognized in the same way as foreign female spouses of Kenyan men.

Yours Sincerely,

Takahashi Hashimoto

William Blake

Dear President Obama,

I am a white American citizen writing to you from the sleepy lakeside town of Kisumu. I joined the letter writing bandwagon quite by chance. Writing to you is probably the greatest thing that has happened to me in a long time. Even if you don't write back, it's quite consoling to know that one's president has heard one's story.

These days, I consider myself to be a rather unlucky character. I wasn't always this negative and pessimistic, but life has made me cynical and even slightly bitter.

You probably won't believe it, but I am a homeless American living on the streets of Kisumu. Yes, that's right. I have nowhere to call home, and I'm literally stranded in this dusty small city in Western Kenya.

I ended up in Kisumu quite by chance about five years ago. I totally blame my arrival in Kisumu on the Internet. Without the Internet, I never would have heard of Club Escapade when on a UN Mission to Kenya, never would have met Maria Ogolla a.k.a Shorty, and never would have ended up stranded in Kisumu.

I am what you could call a former career UN staffer. My UN job had seen me glob trotting for just over a decade when I was posted to the UNEP headquarters in Gigiri, Nairobi. I arrived in Nairobi with a sense of excitement and adventure, eager to explore and enjoy my surroundings. After settling into my new apartment, I eagerly scoured the Internet for clubs in Nairobi. Having identified one, I set out in pursuit of fun and pleasure which I found in the form of Maria from Kisumu.

Unfortunately, Maria turned out to be a con woman. She was greatly obsessed with money as I discovered after leaving my new job. I invested all of my savings on a get rich quick scheme hatched up by Maria, foolishly bought a house in her name, and finally found myself broke and alone on the potholed streets of Kisumu.

I must admit that drugs and alcohol also contributed to my predicament. I've been known to over indulge. Alcohol has a way of confusing even the most intelligent of persons, and totally blurring one's perception of reality. The irony is that I can't even afford a drink these days. I smoke the occasional cigarrete when one of my street buddies feels generous enough to offer a broke mzungu a puff.

Mr. President, I now speak Dholuo much better than that Dutch Catholic priest who occasionally stops by my regular hideout to buy me a plate of fries. He worries a lot about me, and says he's saving to buy me a ticket back to the States. The problem is, I've lost my passport and I'm residing illegally in Kenya. My visa expired more than two years ago. I just don't care anymore. What will be will be.

Oh, I haven't explained how I got to write this letter. This guy called Willis Otieno who sells DVDs claims that his mother is your cousin. Well, Willis recently returned from his mother's home village all excited. He informed me that the residents of Kogelo were writing to you and thought you'd want to hear my story.

Willis is a pretty decent chap. He stops by my street corner to chat in between hawking his DVDs and has bought me lunch more times than I care to remember. Anyway, after I finish writing the letter, I will gave it to Willis who will then dispatch it off to Kogelo by bus. I hope you receive it.

Yours Sincerely,

William Blake

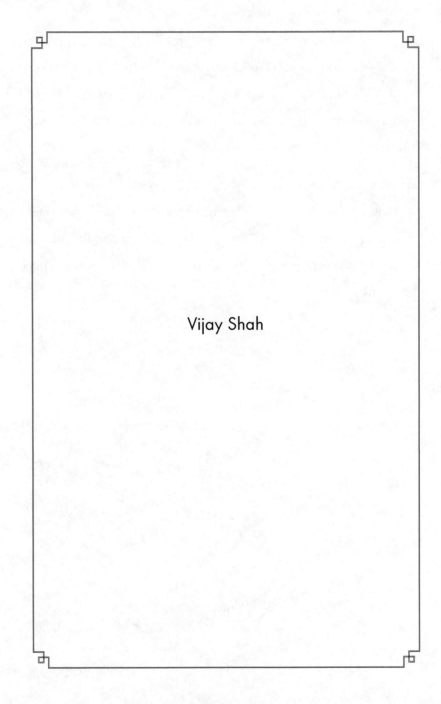

Vijay Shah

Dear Sir,

I hope this finds you well. My name is Vijay Shah, and I'm a Kenyan of Indian ethnicity. It's a great pleasure to write to you.

President Obama, my great grandfather was one of the Indian coolies who worked on the Kenya Uganda railway. Upon the completion of the railway, he settled down in Port Florence, now known as Kisumu and sent for an Indian bride from Rajasthan. Bapa invited his brothers to join him in Kisumu, and together they started Sabuni Industries, a soap factory which is now managed by me and my brothers.

Mr. President, I am writing to you under very strange circumstances. A few weeks ago, my family forcibly brought me to Siaya for treatment by Wuod Petro, a renowned healer from the Roho Safi sect. Wuod Peter is known for healing people with mental disorders many of whom he says are demonically possessed or have been bewitched. President, I am neither mentally unwell nor demonically possessed or bewitched.

My problems began about a year ago when a young Luo lady named Christabel joined Sabuni Industries as our marketing manager. Christabel had previously worked at a Nairobi firm in the same position. She responded to an ad we had placed in the Daily Nation, was interviewed by our uncle Deepak in Nairobi on our behalf, and consequently relocated to Kisumu to take up the position.

My brothers and I tend to keep a professional distance from our female employees though it was impossible to do so with Christabel. She was beautiful, outspoken, outgoing and full of excellent ideas.

At this point, I think I should emphasize the fact that I am a single man and only twenty six years old. I am the last born in a family of four. Unlike my siblings, I have many black Kenyan friends. After primary school, I attended Kisumu Boys High School and forged strong friendships with my classmates most of whom were Luos, Luhyias and Kisiis. After high school, I pursued a degree in Business Administration at the University of London. I later returned to Kisumu to join the family business.

I am currently engaged to an Indian girl called Jyoti whose family responded to a marriage ad my family placed on my behalf in an Indian matchmaking magazine. Jyoti lives in Madras, India with her family. I met her last year when I visited India with my parents to discuss our wedding plans. She is a beautiful young Indian lady from a wealthy family and a good match by all means.

Unfortunately, I don't love Jyoti one bit. That in itself should not constitute a problem since my dad says he was not in love with my mum either when he married her. He says he later grew to love her deeply. He expects that I too will grow to love Jyoti and enjoy many years with her. However, that is unlikely to happen. I am in love with Christabel, a black Luo girl, and she's in love with me.

Mr. President, my first date with Christabel was a business lunch. We were scheduled to meet Mr. Mohammed, a Ugandan businessman at Imperial Hotel, Kisumu. Mr. Mohammed was interested in being the sole distributor of Sabuni products in Uganda. Fortunately or unfortunately, he missed his connecting flight from Nairobi which is how Christabel and I ended up lingering over lunch and drinks until sunset.

We talked about this and that, and really nothing much. Mostly we just enjoyed each other's company. I wondered why I hadn't really noticed Christabel before. She was truly beautiful. Her bright eyes glowed with intelligence in her soft dark skin. She had tiny dimples which appeared when she smiled. Her long braids cascaded down her back and swayed when she moved. She had a tiny waist with broad hips and long legs. She was hot. A true African beauty. Best of all, she had the wit of a judge, the patience of a saint, and the kindness of an angel.

Needless to say, Christabel and I continued to meet in secret after that first date. Kisumu is a very small town so we had to be very careful so as to avoid being detected by members of the local Indian community. Sometimes, we drove out of town to spend the day together. Sometimes we hang out in Christabel's apartment, and sometimes we just sat in my car, chatted all afternoon and listened to music. Meeting at my house was out of the question since I lived with my parents. Once, we "accidentally "ran into each other on the dance floor at a popular nightclub and danced until dawn. We had fun!

All hell broke loose one day when I accidentally kissed Christabel on the lips at the office not knowing that my elder brother Raju was watching us. That evening there was an "intervention" at home the likes of which I'd never seen before.

Papa was shouting, Mama was wailing, my brothers were begging, my sisters-in law were praying, my cousin was sneering, and my grandmother just lay on the carpet speechless. Upset beyond words, I ran upstairs and locked myself in my bedroom. Breakfast the next morning was torture. No one spoke, no one looked me in the eye. Communal living can be terrible!

When I got to the office, Christabel was gone. Raju had fired her. I couldn't talk to her because her phone number was out of service. When I went to her home, her landlady told me she had vacated the apartment the previous evening and hadn't left a forwarding address. Apparently she had been escorted out of the property by two Indian men.

The other girls at work said they didn't know how to trace Christabel since she hadn't discussed her personal life with them. All they knew was that she was from Alego, and had grown up somewhere in Nairobi's Eastlands area. My Christabel had disappeared without a trace. She'd been ran out of town by my brothers. I went mad with rage.

Mr. President, after leaving Christabel's apartment, I rushed to the office driving so fast that I almost drove into a tree opposite Aga Khan Hospital. My brothers were huddled over their computers when I burst into the office we shared in the back of the factory overlooking Lake Victoria.

I started with Vinod. Pulling him from the rear, I turned him around and slapped him hard on the face. He landed heavily on the floor cradling his cheek as tears flowed from his eyes. Next, I landed a flying kick on Raju's back screaming obscenities. His chair rolled round and round as if it had a life of its own. Raju tumbled out of the chair and landed on his knees. I started pulling files off the shelves, tearing documents randomly, and breaking anything and everything I could get my hands on. It took five workers to restrain me.

Dr. Patel our family doctor who had been summoned by my brothers came rushing into the office to sedate me. I fell into a deep slumber. When I woke up, I was in a strange bed in a hot stuffy room. It wasn't my usual bedroom. I was curious but not afraid. I later learnt that I was at Wuod Petro's Roho Safi Healing Centre in Siaya.

My family's trusted and long serving Luo houseboy Mzee Ouma upon hearing the whole story, had convinced Papa that I had been bewitched by the Alego girl, and that the only solution was to take me to Alego for spiritual healing immediately since as they say in Swahili, dawa ya moto ni moto. (The cure for fire is fire).

I've now been here in Siaya for three long weeks. Treatment consists of long prayerful chants in a room full of candles of varied lengths and assorted colors. Incense burns in my room around the clock, and there's a Bible under my pillow. I bathe in "holy water" thrice a day and drink two spoons of the same concoction three times a day.

The Roho Safi are not good cooks. Their food is driving me crazy, literally. Once a day, Wuod Petro the prophet whips me with a cross to drive away the demons. In order for this to happen, I have to be restrained by four robe wearing, cross yielding, rosary chanting Roho Safi brothers with dirty long dreadlocks. Hygiene is a matter of concern here. I'm afraid of getting typhoid.

So why don't I "recover" and leave this place? Well, as fate would have it, Christabel the love of my life has managed to locate me here quite by chance. After being fired by my brother and threatened with death, she decided to retreat to her ancestral home in Kogelo to spend some time with her grandmother Magdalina.

A few days after Christabel arrived in the village, one of her cousins told her he'd heard roumers that there was a Muhindi (Indian) patient at Wuod Petro's. He said, the Indian, a young man was alleged to have been bewitched by a beauty from Alego, and had been sent to the Roho Safi Center for spiritual healing.

Fearing the worst, Christabel decided to investigate this story. She came to the healing center and convinced one of the Roho Safi sisters to allow her into my room. What a reunion. We hugged, and cried, and talked and then cried some more.

One things is for sure, there's no turning back. We are moving forward on our own. My family and my community may shun me for marrying a black Kenyan but I'm not alone. I have a lovely bride by my side. Her people will be my people even if mine won't be hers.

I inherited a good amount of money from Bapa when he passed on three years ago, and it's in my account at the Bank of Baroda. Being an enterprising Indian, I will invest that wisely for my wife and the future Kogelo Indians, our kids.

This afternoon, Christabel and I will walk out of this healing center, and God help any Roho Safi brother who tries to stop us. There's a bunch of village youth by the gate waiting to come to our rescue if need be, and they have plenty of grudges against the Roho Safi. For now, I am working on this letter which Christabel says I must write. It will make her grandmother happy.

Yours Sincerely,

Vijay Shah

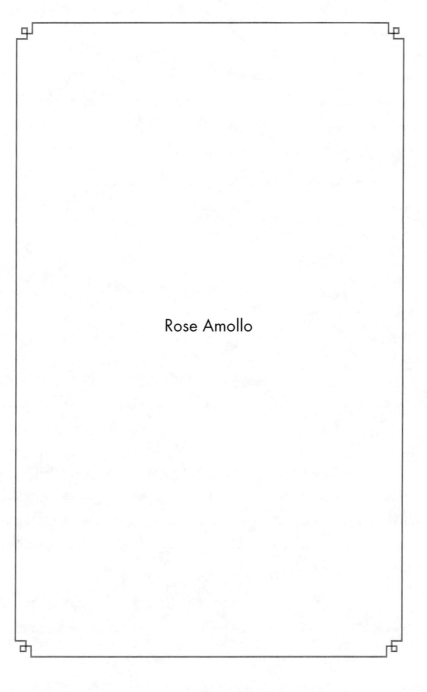

Rose Amollo

Dear President,

My name is Rose Amollo, and I am a housemaid, commonly referred to by Kenyans as "mboch." I recently learnt from my employer's teenage daughter that the term mboch arose from the tem houseboy coined by British colonists for their male house servants. This was shortened by the Brits to "boy" regardless of the servant's age. The term was then generalized by Kenyans to "mboi", and finally "mboch". Years after independence, Kenyans now use this term to refer to their housemaids.

Anyway, Mr. President, I am a mboch and I work in South C Estate in Nairobi. South C is a middle class neighborhood, and my employers are well off. My boss is a doctor while his wife runs a clothes boutique in the neighborhood shopping center. She travels to Turkey and Dubai on a regular basis to purchase stock for her boutique.

I consider myself to be lucky in many ways. I earn a salary of 5000 Kenya shillings which is approximately 56 usd per month. I have a small room to myself, and I am well fed by my employer. Every month, I send two thousand shillings home to my mother in Kogelo. I use 1000 shillings to buy sanitary pads, body lotion and occasionally some second hand clothes and shoes. I save 2000 shillings for my future. My aim is to open a small boutique in about a years' time. I've already saved 20,000 Kenya shillings. My boutique will not be as fancy as my employer's. It will be a sunshine (open air) boutique in one of Nairobi's slums. I will sell used clothes, shoes and handbags.

Mr. President, I have already calculated the cost of my estimated opening stock and set up expenses as follows:

100 pcs of used clothes @ 80 Kshs	8,000
100 used panties and bras @ 10 Kshs	1,000
30 prs used shoes@ 200 Kshs	6,000
20 pcs used handbags @ 100 Kshs	2,000
Renting space at Laini Saba Market	2,000
Total	19,000

Mr. President, I will buy these items dirt cheap from a Somali woman who brings regular shipments of used clothing in by container from Mombasa. I will mark up the prices considerably, so I will end selling everything for a 300% profit.

I'll have to leave my job in order to start my business but that's okay. I'll rent my own room in Kibera Laini Saba for 1000 Kshs per month. I already have a mattress, bed sheets, a cooker, cutlery and a few other household items. I've been buying them slowly.

Mr. President, I am writing to request you to appeal to Kenyan to respect their house maids and treat them well. There are literally hundreds of thousands of house maids all across the country yet our profession is unregulated. Most of us are underpaid in addition to which we work long hours and often get no time off from work to rest. We help to run the wheels of the Kenyan economy by taking care of households so that skilled men and women can go out into the workforce to build the nation. We have brought up generations of Kenyan children while their parents worked in offices and run our government.

To the house maids out there, my message is that we should represent ourselves well, and conduct ourselves professionally. We should avoid stealing from our employers, abusing children, and misusing resources. We should not work for people who abuse us. Every housemaid should make an effort to save for the future. We can all have a better future. "Tunawesmake."

Yours Sincerely.

Rose Amollo Nyar Kogelo

Hamid Abdullahi

Dear President Obama,

I greet you in the name of Allah. My name is Hamid Abdullahi and I am a Kenyan Somali. I was born in Maralal but later moved to Nairobi's Eastleigh Estate where I attended school and grew up amongst Kenyan and refugee Somalis. I am currently a trader at Garissa Lodge in Eastleigh. I sell perfumes, hijabs, handbags, incense, cosmetics and ladies shoes. Most of my customers are working class Kenyan women who throng my stall at the end of the month to spend their hard earned cash on beauty products.

Mr. President, I must admit that it's kind of hard being a Kenyan today. Growing up, I was proud of my identity as a Kenyan Somali, now I'm mostly afraid. I feel guilty even though I've done nothing wrong. I feel that people don't trust me anymore. Although they try to keep their voices low, I hear their whispers. Many people assume that I am a Somali refugee, so they talk about me in Kiswahili. Of course I understand everything they say and it hurts me a lot. It wasn't this way when I was young. My people were mostly respected and appreciated. Now everyone's afraid of us.

I don't know what to say except that I wish my fellow Kenyans the very best. I pray for peace and security every day, and trust that by the grace of Allah, Kenyans will be able to shop, travel, work, and study safely without fear.

I wish you a pleasant visit to Kenya.

Yours Sincerely,

Hamid Abdullahi

Leah Konchellah

Dear President Obama,

I am writing to you from the heart of Texas where I currently reside. I am a Maasai girl from Kajiado but have lived in the United States for over a decade now. I came here to pursue an undergraduate degree in nursing with the hopes of eventually entering the American workforce, becoming a citizen of the US of A, and realizing the American Dream.

My dream has come true to an extent. I am part of the American workforce, but I am one of the many who are referred to as undocumented aliens. You see, my original student visa expired years ago, and I ended up throwing away my passport in a bid to escape identification and possible apprehension and deportation.

These days, I'm like a phantom. Now you see me, now you don't. I've got so many identities, even I get confused. My current employer thinks I'm Uche, a 24 year old Nigerian student. Apparently, we Africans all look alike age notwithstanding

Mr. President, my life in America hasn't been all bread and butter. Far from it. I work too hard, spend too much, save too little, and jump at my own shadow now that I'm officially illegal. I feel trapped in many ways.

There are many Kenyans here in Texas and that makes me feel at home. However, I find myself thinking of Kenya more and more frequently. I miss my friends and family and feel hopeless because I don't know when and if I'll ever step on Kenyan soil again. I'd give anything to see my grandmother's toothless smile, and to taste my mother's cooking

You're probably wondering why I don't board a plane and return home. I've thought of returning home countless times but something keeps holding me back, something that I've come to acknowledge as fear, the fear of becoming a failure. Trust me, it's easy to become one in Kenya.

Mr. President, I never finished my degree in nursing. That's right. All I have is a high school certificate. I am a product of that age when Kenyan parents sent their kids to the States without adequate tuition fees, and asked them to work hard and pay their way through college. Apparently, it worked and still works for some. It didn't work for me maybe because I was constantly bombarded with requests for money from home. First it was a wedding, then a funeral, then tuition fees for my siblings, then my parent's rent.

The bills kept arriving, and I kept running to Western Union. The next thing I knew, I was unable to keep up with my tuition fees and ended up deciding to drop out of college to pursue fulltime employment and send more money home. Shortly after that, my legal status in the US expired. Now, I'm stuck between a rock and a hard place - being illegal in the US or jobless in Kenya. That's a no brainer.

A second reason why I can't go home is because I don't have any investments back there. It goes without saying that Kenyans expect their brethren abroad to invest in something – anything. One is expected to buy land, build a house, and possibly invest in some kind of income generating activity all of which provide a safety net for returning diaspora. Well, I've got none of the listed items. How do you invest when you're bankrolling an entire clan of people? The same people who would laugh at you if you returned home and ended up jobless and homeless. That is so not happening to me. I'd rather be homeless in America. Okay, forget I said that.

Mr. President, there's yet another barrier to my returning home. My children who are legal citizens of the States. Trey is seven and so cute. Lakisha is four and fabulous. I love my kids. I would do anything for them. The kids share a daddy. An American man who is no longer in my life. The last I heard, someone said they saw him on MSNBC's "Lock Up." Apparently, he's in jail in Florida. Don't ask me why.

Tom was pretty nice to me before I had the second baby. He had a decent well-paying job too. Then he said he was going to Florida on business. He didn't say what kind of business, and he never came back. My kids keep asking about their daddy but there's no way I'm telling them their dad is a convicted felon.

President Obama, one of my best friends here is from Siaya. Unlike me, she is a legal resident of the United States. A holder of that coveted document called a green card. She recently returned from Kenya full of ideas of projects that we can invest in at home. She thinks a large scale ecotourism project in the villages around Lake Victoria would be both sustainable and profitable. I agree with her. We are currently looking for American venture capitalists to fund our ideas. If this works, I'm returning home to Kenya forever. That Mr. President is my new American Dream.

Yours Sincerely,

Leah Konchellah

Elijah Nyangweso

Dear Sir,

I feel really privileged to be able to write to you. All my life I've wanted to share my experiences with the world. I feel that writing to you is a pathway to being heard. If you are moved by what I have to say, maybe you will share it with the global community.

Mr. President, my name is Elijah Nyangweso, and I am a Kisii tribesman from Nyamira in Western Kenya. I am a game warden by profession. I work for the Wildlife Police Services (WPS) and have been stationed at the Maasai Mara National Park for the last twenty years in which I've had life changing experiences.

Mr. President, this place has made me in many ways. It has also changed me beyond recognition, not only physically but also mentally and emotionally. Sometimes I stare at myself in the mirror, and wonder who I really am.

My journey into the world of wildlife began after I graduated from Archbishop Onyancha High School, better known as "Archs." Since I didn't qualify to join a university, I applied for a job at WPS and was surprisingly fortunate to land an interview and later a job. It's so hard to get a job in Kenya that it's actually surprising when you get one easily without help from a friend or relative, or without money exchanging hands.

Heh! My first year at WPS wasn't easy. Bush trekking, mountain climbing, thorns in the bush, cactus, the hot scorching sun, hailstones, sand storms, insect bites, snake bites and worst or best of all, the beasts of the bush.

Being a wildlife warden just doesn't grow on you. You learn, you suffer, you try and fail, and then you try again until you become one with the jungle. The first time I returned home on leave from work, my mum couldn't believe her eyes. She said my face had been blackened beyond recognition, and that my hands were hard and calloused. She demanded that I resign from my job and help my dad to grow coffee on our ever shrinking plantation. I said no, and thus sealed my fate.

Mr. President, as I mentioned earlier on, the Maasai Mara has shaped my life in many ways. That's where I met my wife Kwamboka. I was a twenty three year old trigger happy game warden, she was a twenty year old pretty waitress. We met one fine day in July, quite by accident. The Camp Manager at Tembo Kubwa Safari Lodge called our station to report a rogue elephant which was bent on destroying his lodge by tearing down tents and uprooting trees. Nothing would make it leave so they called us.

When I got to the camp. I immediately noticed what the problem was. Something had disturbed the bee hives that were located on the huge jacaranda trees along the park's entrance driveway. Consequently, the bees were swarming all over the area just outside

Tembo Kubwa. The irate elephant had sensed the imminent danger from the bees and just wouldn't budge. Strange to think that such a huge animal would fear such tiny insects. Needless to say, we got rid of the bees, and the elephant left the lodge and its fearful residents.

It took us six hours to get rid of the bees and the elephant which we nicknamed Njoki. When the drama was over, my team and I were invited to have dinner with John Smith the Lodge Manager which is how I met Kwamboka my lovely wife.

Kwamboka and I exchanged long glances over osso buco and grilled potatoes which she served us gracefully. As we left, I found an excuse to linger in the dining hall under the pretext of making an inquiry. I slipped Kwamboka a note with my phone number as I walked out, and from then on, we texted night and day until she became my wife.

Mr. President, the other significant relationship that I developed that day was with Njoki, the elephant. It was almost as though destiny was beckoning me, as though yin and yang had revealed themselves.

My wedding day was approaching. Kwamboka was already on leave in Kisii planning the wedding from the comfort of her ancestral home in Keroka. I was still out there in the bush, working hard and trying to save up for the wedding which was scheduled to take place at Kisii SDA Central. Kwamboka, my lovely gracious wife insisted that we hold a small wedding. She said it was important not to live beyond our means. She even suggested that we have a small civil wedding and do away with a church wedding.

I would have none of that. My cousin Simon had recently returned home from Minnesota for his wedding which had been extremely colorful and which had been attended by relatives from all corners of the globe.

Simon had always been my rival though we had a lot in common. Our fathers were brothers. We both loved and hated each other. We'd both studied at "Archs", we'd both failed to get admitted into a university in Kenya. We knew we'd both inherit our ancestral shamba being the only sons of our fathers who had in turn been the only sons of their father. We both knew we wanted more than an 8 acre coffee farm.

Fortunately for Simon, his mother's sister's sister- in-law's husband was a pastor in the United States. My uncle beseeched Simon's mum, who blackmailed her sister, who wrote to her sister-in-law, who persuaded the pastor, who pulled some strings which landed my dear cousin in the US of A. I ended up in the lovely but dangerous and mysterious Maasai Mara. So far from home yet so near.

So how does a Kenyan game warden compete with a medical assistant who works multiple hours and earns "Benjamins" in St. Paul Minnesota? Wise men say God helps those who help themselves, so I started to help myself.

A week after Njoki had invaded and messed up Tembo Kubwa Lodge, I was sleeping in my cubicle at the KWS camp when I was woken up by the cackling of my walkie talkie. It was my buddy Owiti. He and some of the guys were approximately ten kilometers away, somewhere near the Kenya Tanzania border. They were working with a team of researchers and basically helping them to dart and sedate wildlife which would then be tagged for the purposes of tracking for research. The animals would later be released into the wild. Owiti and his team needed an extra hand, and so I jumped into a WPS Jeep and drove off to find them.

A few meters away from the WPS camp, I noticed something suspicious. A jungle green off road vehicle was snaking its way towards the Mara River. It was way off the beaten track that's usually used by tour operators and WPS officers. It was heading towards a water hole that's known to only those that are very familiar with the Mara, namely local Maasai morans and people like myself. Sensing mischief, I swiftly changed course and followed the jungle green vehicle which turned out to be an extremely well equipped Range Rover.

Mr. President, the men in that vehicle were very clever. Apparently, they had spotted me and had sent a driver ahead as a diversion while several of them disembarked and placed a barrier of thick thorns across the path thus causing me to suddenly halt. That's when they ambushed me. I was drugged and carried off into the bush.

When I regained consciousness, I was in the middle of an abandoned Maasai manyatta with no Maasai in sight. The place smelt of cow dung and sour cow urine. There were flies everywhere and several carcasses of dead animals. Several vultures hovered in the sky. I wondered if I was alive. I soon realized that I was when a hot slap landed on my face followed by a disgusting gob of spit which splattered on my forehead.

A short Chinese man stood over me, a black pistol in his hand. A ferocious looking tall black man towered over us all carrying a sharp machete. I was so scared I peed on myself. I cursed the day I had applied for a job at WPS. Somewhere in the near distance, an evil looking mzungu chewed on a toothpick while two turbaned Arabs watched us in amusement. A Sikh in a Kaunda suit pranced nervously around the manyatta conversing on a sophisticated looking mobile phone. What were these assorted characters doing here in the middle of nowhere?

The Chinese man informed me that they had a proposition for me which had only two possible outcomes; great wealth or instant death. He did not mince his words, and I could see that he meant every single word that came out of his mouth.

I chose great wealth. I joined that ring of poachers, and gave Kwamboka a fancy wedding after hunting down and shooting Njoki and the herd of elephants that she grazed with. All of this was done while I was still on the payroll of WPS. Unbeknown to my bosses, the enemy was now in their midst.

Twenty years later, I am still both a game warden and a poacher. I cannot escape the Mara because here is where I make my dough. Also, I know too much and Chen Hui and his friends both white and black will never let me go.

Kwamboka is still my wife. My precious girl from Keroka. She is the one thing that I hold dear in this world. She's a nice person and is totally devoted to the church. She's given me three lovely children all of whom are in Minnesota because my wife...No, we didn't need to call or beg or write to anyone. We have money, and the kids applied and got admitted to universities which I pay for using proceeds from my "business."

The animals. Their blood cries out to me and I see them in my dreams. Through the years, my friends and I have slaughtered thousands of elephants, rhinos, lions and other precious animals.

I own a huge mansion on the outskirts of Kisii town. My wife drives a Pajero and runs a hotel. She went back to Utalii College and earned herself a diploma in hospitality. She's still very beautiful. Kwamboka thinks I borrowed money to build that luxurious hotel. Poor innocent thing. She doesn't realize that she's living off the fat of the Mara, that her beloved husband is a great slaughterer of the Big Five, that I am a poacher.

How can Kwamboka not suspect a thing? Is she really that ignorant? My fellow game wardens still sleep in huts when they come home for Christmas! They are really honorable chaps. All of them except for Owiti who I recruited into the game. He now has five wives and owns many businesses in Migori and Homa Bay. We are the kings of South Nyanza. God helps those who help themselves. I wonder what Njoki thinks looking down on me from elephant heaven. I guess I'll find out some day.

Kind Regards.

Elijah

As I Grew Older

It was a long time ago.

I have almost forgotten my dream.

But it was there then,

In front of me,

Bright like a sun—

My dream.

And then the wall rose,

Rose slowly,

Slowly,

Between me and my dream.

Rose until it touched the sky—

The wall.

Shadow.

I am black.

I lie down in the shadow.

No longer the light of my dream before me,

Above me.

Only the thick wall.

Only the shadow.

My hands!

My dark hands!

Break through the wall!

Find my dream!

Help me to shatter this darkness,

To smash this night,

To break this shadow

Into a thousand lights of sun,

Into a thousand whirling dreams

Of sun!

Langston Hughes

Printed in the United States
By Bookmasters